Acknowledgements

Writing *The Art of Desire* has been a journey of emotion, imagination and vulnerability. My deepest gratitude goes to everyone who encouraged me to bring this story to life. To those who believed in the tenderness between Madeline and Geneviève, thank you for seeing the beauty in their forbidden world.

To my friends and readers - your enthusiasm, curiosity and kindness mean more than words. And to anyone who has ever chosen their own truth over expectations, this story is for you.

Thank you for turning these pages with an open heart.

CHAPTER ONE
The Announcement

The morning sun spilled across the polished marble floors of the de Marais estate, gilding everything it touched - goblets, gowns and the expectant faces of the assembled guests. Madeline sat at the edge of the velvet-cushioned chair, hands folded in her lap like a porcelain doll.
Her mother had chosen the pale blue dress for the occasion, claiming it brought out the innocence in her eyes.

She felt anything but innocent as she sat there feeling the nervousness and resentment rise within her from the pit of her stomach.

The drawing room buzzed with polite conversation, the kind that masked judgment behind lace fans and laughter. Her Father - the Marquis stood near the hearth, his voice booming with pride.

"An alliance of great fortune and legacy," he declared. "Our daughter Madeline, will be wed to Étienne de Villeroy before the harvest moon."

A ripple of approval passed through the room. Madeline's stomach turned.

Étienne, seated beside her - offered a smile that didn't even reach his eyes. He was handsome - certainly, with golden curls, a jaw carved from ambition - but there was something hollow in his gaze, as if he saw her not as a woman - but as a ledger entry and a future trophy.

She nodded politely, the way she'd been taught. Smile. Tilt your head. Say nothing.

Madeline had only met Étienne a handful of times over the last few months, he showed little interest in getting to know her as a person and was always eager to leave her side to discuss business with her Father. She could feel how ruthless he had the potential to be - and what little care he had for her and her happiness as his future Wife.

~ ~ ~

The next morning in the quiet of her chamber, Madeline stood before the mirror and studied her reflection. The girl in the glass looked composed, serene.
But beneath the surface, a storm brewed - she felt helpless to remove herself from her proposed future but something inside her told her not to give up hope.

A knock at the door.

Her maid entered, curtsying. "Madame Rousseau has arrived. She awaits you in the east salon."

Madeline blinked. "Who?"

"Your tutor," the maid replied. "For your...your preparation."

The word hung in the air like perfume - sweet, strange and slightly suffocating.

Over the last few months her Mother had mentioned that there would be someone brought to the house to help her "prepare" for married life and all the expectations that involved - but now the moment was here she felt scared and unsure of what this would actually involve and especially since her dislike for Étienne was growing and growing after each meeting.

Madeline walked the cold corridors and descended the staircase slowly that led to the salon, each step echoing with uncertainty. Madeline hesitated at the threshold, her fingers grazing the carved wood of the open doorframe.

The east salon was dimly lit, its windows draped in crimson velvet. A woman stood by the fireplace, her silhouette framed by flickering light.

She turned.

Madeleine Rousseau was unlike anyone Madeline had ever seen. Older - yes, but not aged.

Her beauty was quiet, deliberate, dark eyes and almost black hair. She had a presence that filled the room without a word.

Madeline curtsied. "Madame."

Geneviève gestured to a chair near the hearth. "Sit, child."

Madeline obeyed, smoothing her skirts as she perched on the edge of the seat. Her posture was perfect, her chin lifted just so - years of etiquette drilled into her bones. But her hands trembled slightly in her lap.

Geneviève watched her with a gaze that was neither indulgent nor critical. It was…curious. As though she were studying a painting whose meaning had not yet revealed itself.

"You are afraid," she said, not unkindly.

Madeline stiffened. "I'm not…I…"

"You are," Geneviève interrupted, gently. "And you should be. Fear is not weakness. It is the body's way of telling the soul to pay attention."

Madeline blinked, unsure how to respond. No one had ever spoken to her like this - certainly not her Mother, whose words were always wrapped in duty and decorum.

Geneviève smiled, and it was not the smile of courtly etiquette. It was something else - something that saw through silk and ceremony.

Geneviève moved to a small table and poured tea from a porcelain pot. The cups were thin and painted with violets. She handed one to Madeline, who accepted it with a murmured thank you.

"I am here to teach you," she said softly. "But not only what your family expects."

Madeline's breath caught.

"They think I am here to teach you how to please a man," Geneviève said, settling into the chair opposite. "That is what they expect. That is something I am certainly capable of but first I will teach you how to know yourself. How to listen to the voice that has been whispering inside you since you were a girl."

Geneviève stepped closer. "I am here to teach you what it means to know pleasure. To be seen and see yourself. To be known and to know yourself."

Madeline's throat tightened. "What if I can't do this? "

Geneviève's smile returned, slow and enigmatic. "You can do this Madeline - but we start slowly, searching within the silence to find the truth that lives in your heart and mind."

They sat for a moment, the fire crackling between them, the tea untouched.

Geneviève leaned forward. "Tell me, Madeline. When you look in the mirror...what do you see?"

Madeline glanced toward the tall glass across the room, its surface now dimmed by shadow. "A girl who has always done what she must do."

"And beneath that?"

Madeline's voice was barely a whisper. "A girl who doesn't want to."

Geneviève nodded, as if this were the answer she had been waiting for.

"Good," she said. "Then we have something real to work with."

Outside, the bells of the cathedral rang. Inside, something far more sacred had begun…

After Madeline left, Geneviève sat alone in the east salon, the fire reduced to embers. She picked up a velvet box that lay closed on the table, its contents untouched. She had used them many times before - tools of instruction, of transformation. But tonight, they felt different. More personal.

Madeline de Marais…

The name echoed in her mind like a bell tolling in a cathedral. So young, so tightly wound in silk and silence. Yet behind those wide eyes, Geneviève had seen something flicker - curiosity, defiance, hunger.

She poured herself a glass of wine, the deep red liquid catching the firelight. She had taught many girls. Some were frightened. Some were eager. None had looked at her the way Madeline had - when their eyes met - they locked and lingered and for the first time Geneviève did not feel as if she were the tutor, but a question which Madeline longed to know the answer.

Geneviève ran her fingers through her hair and thought of all the years she had spent merely surviving. She had vowed never to feel again. Never to want. But Madeline's presence had stirred something dormant in her - a tenderness she had buried beneath years of control.

She closed her eyes.

This cannot happen, she told herself.

But the heart is not a servant. It does not obey.

CHAPTER TWO

The First Lesson

The next morning the east salon was quiet, save for the soft ticking of the gilded clock and the distant rustle of leaves beyond the window. Madeleine stood at the threshold, uncertain. Geneviève sat in a high-backed chair, her posture elegant, her gaze unreadable.

"Come in," she said firmly but not unkindly.

Madeleine obeyed, her slippers whispering against the floor. She felt like a child summoned to recite a lesson, though the subject was one she'd never imagined.

Geneviève gestured to the chaise across from her. "Sit."

Madeleine did, smoothing her skirts with trembling fingers.

"You've been taught how to walk, how to speak, how to smile," Geneviève said. "But not how to feel."

Madeleine blinked. "Feel?"

Geneviève leaned forward, her voice low. "Desire. Pleasure. Power. These are not sins, Madeleine. They are human nature and they are truths. You must learn them before you give yourself to a man who may never ask what you want."

Madeleine's throat tightened. "What if I don't know what I want?"

Geneviève smiled, gently. "That is what I am here for, to find out what you want and to help you recognise it for yourself."

She rose and crossed the room, retrieving the small velvet box from the cabinet. Inside were objects Madeleine didn't recognise - silks, oils, a carved ivory comb, a feather amongst other items. Geneviève placed them on the table between them like offerings.

"These are tools," she said. "But they mean nothing without understanding your own body."

Madeleine flushed. "What do you mean?..."

"I mean," Geneviève said. "I will be showing you not only how to give pleasure but how to feel pleasure, although that is not the lesson today.

She handed Madeleine a mirror - oval, silver-framed, cool in her hands.

Today you will learn to see yourself."

Madeleine swallowed hard, she was only just starting to comprehend what these lessons were about, something that had never been talked about her entire sheltered life and it was stirring emotions and sensations in her that she had never experienced.

"Tonight, when you are alone, look. Not as a future bride. Not as a Daughter, but as a woman."

Madeleine stared at the mirror, her reflection pale and wide-eyed.

Geneviève voice softened. "There is no shame in knowing yourself Madeline. Only power."

They sat in silence, the air between them thick with something unnamed. When Madeleine finally looked up, Geneviève was watching her - not with judgment but with something deeper. Recognition.

"You will return tomorrow, if you wish" Geneviève said rising. "and you will tell me what you saw and what you felt."

Madeleine nodded, feeling self conscious and a little terrified as her fingers curled around the mirror.

As she left the salon, the world outside seemed louder, harsher. But inside her, something had shifted. A door had opened and behind it, a question waited - not of duty, but of desire.

~ ~ ~

Madeline closed the door to her chamber with trembling hands and locked it.

The mirror was still in her grasp, its silver frame cool against her palm, its weight heavier than she expected - not in metal but in meaning. She set it gently on the vanity, as if it might shatter from too much power.

The room was quiet. The fire had burned low. Outside, the wind stirred the ivy along the stone walls, whispering secrets she was curious to hear.

She sat at her dresser in front of the mirror, staring at her own reflection. Pale skin. Wide eyes. A mouth that had never spoken of longing - lips that had never been kissed. She looked like a girl still, but something inside her had begun to shift - like silk unraveling from a spool.

Geneviève's words echoed in her mind.

"Not as a bride. Not as a Daughter. But as a woman."

Madeline reached for the candle, lighting it with a trembling match. The flame flickered, casting golden light across her face. She removed her gown slowly, deliberately, as if each button undone was a layer of innocence peeled away.

She stood in her chemise, then slipped it off, letting it fall to the floor like a sigh.

Naked, she sat again.

She looked.

At first, she saw only skin. The curve of her shoulder. The slope of her collarbone. The soft swell of her breasts. But then, she saw more.

She saw the way her body held tension. The way her breath caught when her fingers brushed her own arm. The way her thighs pressed together - but not in shame.

She touched her skin slowly, with a new found respect for her body. Her fingertips traced the lines of her hips, the hollow of her belly, the place between her legs where sensation stirred like a fire.

She didn't rush. She didn't hide.

She watched herself.

And for the first time, she didn't feel like a stranger to her own body.

Tears slipped down her cheeks - these were not tears of sadness but from happiness, hope and a feeling of empowerment that she had never felt before. She was not just a vessel. Not just a promise to be delivered. She was a woman. With hunger. With power. With choice.

She whispered into the candlelight, "I see you."

And the mirror did not flinch.

Later, wrapped in a robe, she lay in bed with the mirror beside her. She didn't sleep for hours. Her body hummed with new knowledge, her mind replaying every word Geneviève had spoken to her.

She had been awakened.

And tomorrow, she would return - as a pupil - yes - but also as someone who had begun to understand the lessons being taught.

CHAPTER THREE

Revelation

The next morning, Madeline stood once again at the threshold of the east salon.

She was changed, though no one else could see it. Her posture was straighter. Her eyes steadier. The mirror had shown her more than her body - it had shown her endless possibility and a whole new world.

Geneviève looked up from her writing desk. Her expression was unreadable at first - then it softened into something almost pride like.

"You returned," she said.

Madeline stepped inside. "Of course. You asked me to."

"I told you only to come if you wished," Geneviève replied.

Madeline stepped closer. "Then I wished it."

Geneviève gestured to the chaise. "Sit. Tell me what you saw"

Madeline hesitated, then lowered herself onto the cushion. "I saw myself and I didn't turn away."

Geneviève's expression softened. "Good."

A quiet smile touched Geneviève's lips.

The fire crackled softly in the grate. Between them, the air seemed to hum - with understanding.

"I want to learn," Madeline said. "Not about rules. About...freedom. About what it means to belong to myself."

Madeline's voice trembled. "I didn't know I could feel that way. I didn't know I was allowed."

Geneviève leaned forward. "You are allowed. You are entitled. Your body is not merely a gift to be given to someone else - it is your home to be inhabited."

Madeline swallowed hard. "I want to learn more."

Geneviève rose and crossed the room, retrieving a silk scarf from the velvet box. She sat beside Madeline this time, closer than before.

"Today," she said, "we begin with sensation."

"This," she said, "is what most mistake for constraint. But in truth, it teaches awareness. Sensation. Presence."

She brushed the fabric across Madeline's open palm. The texture was cool, then warm where it lingered.

She tied the scarf gently around Madeline's wrist, then dragged the fabric slowly across her palm, her forearm, the inside of her elbow. "Every sense is like a language," Geneviève murmured. "The more you listen, the more fluent you become."

"Close your eyes," Geneviève whispered.

Madeline obeyed.

"Pleasure is not only between your thighs," Geneviève said. "It is in your skin, in your mind and in your anticipation."

She placed a drop of scented oil on Madeline's collarbone. The scent bloomed, jasmine, sandalwood and something richer -

darker that she didn't recognise.

Madeline with her eyes closed breathed deeply.

Geneviève's voice was low, steady. "Imagine someone touching you - not taking but giving. Not to claim you but to worship you."

Madeline shivered.

Geneviève continued. "Imagine that person is your future Husband. Or someone you choose. That is the lesson."

Madeline opened her eyes. "I want to choose."

Geneviève met her gaze. "Then choose carefully. And never apologise."

They sat in silence, staring at each other, the scarf still trailing across Madeline's skin, the oil warming her chest, the air between them thick with something electric.

"You are learning to inhabit yourself," she said. "This is what I wanted to teach you."

Madeline nodded. "It feels like remembering something I've forgotten."

Geneviève stood. "Then next, we begin with touch. If you're ready."

Madeline rose slowly. "I think I've been ready longer than I knew."

Geneviève smiled. "Good."

As Madeline turned to leave, she caught her reflection in the tall mirror by the door. The girl she had been was still there - but behind her eyes was a new light. Steady. Aware. Awake.

~ ~ ~

Madeline's Mother had called for her to come see her to discuss how the lessons were progressing. The drawing room was bathed in the mid morning light, the lace curtains casting delicate shadows across the floor. Madeline sat stiffly on the edge of the velvet settee, her hands folded in her lap, the mirror tucked away in her chamber like a secret.

Her Mother, Madame de Marais, poured tea with practiced grace. Not a drop spilled. Not a word spoken.

Finally, she looked up. "You've been very quiet."

Madeline hesitated. "I've been thinking."

Her Mother stirred her tea. "About the wedding?"

Madeline's throat tightened. "About myself."

Madame de Marais raised an eyebrow. "Yourself?"

Madeline nodded. "I've had a couple of lessons with Madame Rousseau."

Her Mother's expression didn't change but her grip on the spoon faltered. "She's unconventional to say the least…but comes highly recommended."

"She's honest," Madeline said. "She asked me what I want."

Her Mother set the spoon down. "And what did you say?"

"I said I didn't know," Madeline whispered. "But I'm starting to."

A silence stretched between them, filled with the ticking of the clock and the distant hum of the garden.

Madame de Marais spoke carefully. "Regardless of what you want. You are to marry Étienne. He is respectable. Wealthy. Well-positioned."

Madeline looked down. "But he doesn't see me or seem to want to know me."

"He doesn't need to," her Mother said. "He needs to provide.

Protect. Preserve your place."

Madeline's voice cracked. "What if I want more than a place?"

Her Mother's eyes softened just for a moment. "Wanting more is dangerous."

Madeline leaned forward. "Did you ever want more?"

Madame de Marais blinked, as if the question had pierced something long buried. She looked away. "Once."

"What happened?"

"I married your Father," she said. "And I learned to want less."

Madeline's heart ached. "I don't want to learn that."

Her Mother stood, smoothing her skirts. "Then you must be very careful, Madeline. The world does not reward women who choose themselves."

Madeline rose too. "Then let it punish me. But I will not be silent."

Madame de Marais turned to her, eyes glistening. "You are brave and I am afraid for you."

Madeline stepped closer. "You don't have to be."

They stood together in the gentle light, two women bound by blood and expectation - one resigned, one awakening.

And though no resolution was spoken, something had shifted.

Madeline had begun to speak.

And her Mother had begun to listen.

CHAPTER FOUR

The Awakening

That evening in the East Salon, Madeline could not wait to see Geneviéve again - it had only been 24 hours but it felt like days and she was eager to continue her lessons and learn more.

Her intrigue in Geneviéve was consuming and she longed to know what she knew.

Geneviève spoke softly to her once she entered the room "You've learned to see yourself. Now you learn to be seen and touched."

Madeline's breath caught and her eyes widened "By you?"

Geneviève nodded. "Only if you allow it."

Madeline looked down at her hands. "Yes of course I do allow it - but I am afraid."

"Of me?" Geneviève asked with concern

"No. Of myself and of what I don't yet know."

Geneviève reached for the oil, warming a few drops between her palms. "Then let me show you that there is nothing to fear."

She touched Madeline's shoulder - lightly. Her fingers moved slowly, tracing the curve of her collarbone, the line of her neck. Madeline closed her eyes, her breath shallow.

"This is not about performance," Geneviève whispered. "It's about being present and feeling what you feel in this moment."

Her hands moved lower, over the silk of Madeline's gown, never rushing, never demanding. Each touch was a question that Madeline silently answered, with her stillness, with the soft tilt of her head.

Geneviève paused. "May I?"

Madeline opened her eyes. "Yes."

Geneviève undid the first clasp of her gown, then the second. The fabric fell away like petals, revealing skin flushed with anticipation. She leaned in, her lips brushing Geneviève's shoulder - not with hunger but with respect.

Madeline trembled. "I've never felt like this."

Geneviève met her gaze. "You've never been allowed to," she said as she reached down and gently took Madeline's hand and led her to the bed.

Geneviève laid her down gracefully and traced her face with her fingers down to her neck, then between her breast continuing to circle them with her fingertips and running her palm over her nipples - Madeline was alive with sensation - this was so much more than she could have ever imagined and her body was responding with sensations she had never felt before.

She felt this should feel weird or unnatural - but she had never wanted anything like this more in her life - and she trusted Geneviève already in the short time that she'd known her.

As Geneviève's fingers continued their journey down Madeline's belly they ever so gently brushed over her pubic bone, causing an involuntary jolt of sensation. Geneviève continued and travelled slowly along the inside of Madeline's thigh and towards her knees.

Madeline shuddered and ached to be touched where she never had before - it was like a throbbing heat between her legs calling

Genevieve's hand to come back and touch her - to relieve her. Geneviève head was hovering only inches away from Madelines aching groin - she looked back up towards Madeline to see her with her head tilted back, her eyes closed and mouth open - gasping in pleasure.

For Geneviève, this lesson had aroused more in her than she had anticipated, she was so stimulated by touching Madeline - this had never happened before and it was something out of her control. She knew from the first moment she met Madeline that something in her was stirred and awakened, but this was unlike anything she had ever experienced. Normally she was so professional but this was causing her to want to loose control and get completely lost in Madeline.

This was unacceptable - she couldn't let this happen - it was unprofessional and dangerous for the both of them.

She stopped abruptly and got up off the bed.

"I think that's enough for today Madeline," she said as she pressed her dress down with her hands.

Madeline looked shocked and dazed as if woken from a dream, "but why - did I do something wrong?"

"No Madeline," Geneviève quickly composed herself so as not to shame Madeline and ruin the progress so far. "I just feel we need to go in stages - there is a lot to learn and it can not all be learnt in one lesson"

Madeline blinked and pulled her gown up around her, she seemed confused with the abrupt end to the lesson and couldn't quite read Geneviève.

"When would you like to see me again?"

"I will call for you Madeline, take some time to let this lesson settle in with you and to continue to explore yourself"

Madeline looked down, disappointed - she wanted more and she did not want to wait. Something in her had stirred so deeply when Geneviève touched her and looked into her eyes - it was like she was looking into her soul.

That evening, Madeline returned to her chambers with her pulse still racing. Every inch of her skin seemed alive with memory - not just of touch but of the nearness, the gentleness, the restraint that had passed between them. She tried to calm her mind, to think of anything else, yet Geneviève's voice echoed through her thoughts like a melody she couldn't forget.

For the first time, she understood that what she felt went far beyond curiosity. It was longing - deep, unfamiliar and impossible to ignore.

Geneviève had awakened something in her that no one, especially not Étienne had ever stirred.

When morning came, the world felt different. Colours seemed sharper and the air felt thicker.

CHAPTER FIVE

The Demand

Étienne de Villeroy had visited the estate three times in the past fortnight since the announcement of the engagement.

Each time, he arrived with fresh flowers, polished boots and the expectation of being received. And each time he was met with the same reply:

"Madeline regrets she cannot join you. She is occupied with her preparations and lessons."

At first, he was patient. After all, the wedding was approaching and he understood the importance of preparation. But by the third visit, his patience had soured from rejection - something he was not used to.

He paced the drawing room, his fingers drumming against the arm of the settee. "Lessons," he muttered. "What could possibly require such secrecy?"

The butler entered. "Would you care for tea, Monsieur?"

Étienne waved him off. "No. I will speak with Monsieur de Marais. Now."

The butler hesitated, then bowed. "As you wish."

Minutes later, Madeline's Father entered the room, his expression unreadable.

Étienne stood. "Forgive the intrusion, but I must speak plainly."

Monsieur de Marais gestured for him to sit. "Go on."

"I am to marry your Daughter in less than a month," Étienne said. "And yet I have barely seen her. She avoids me. She claims to be busy with lessons but I suspect there is more."

Monsieur de Marais raised an eyebrow. "You suspect what, exactly?"

"That she is being influenced," Étienne said. "By Madame Rousseau. The tutor."

Monsieur de Marais's gaze sharpened. "She is here to prepare Madeline for marriage."

Étienne leaned forward. "Then let her prepare her for me - her future husband! I request - no - I insist on - a private visit. Tomorrow. No excuses."

Monsieur de Marais considered him for a long moment. "You are her Fiancé. You are entitled to speak with her."

Étienne stood. "Then I shall return tomorrow at noon."

He bowed stiffly and left the room, his boots echoing down the corridor.

Upstairs, Madeline sat at her writing desk, the mirror tucked beneath a silk scarf, her journal open to a blank page. She had heard Étienne's voice through the floorboards - sharp, demanding and it made her shiver - for all the wrong reasons.

All she could think of was Geneviéve and how she had touched her and how she needed to see her again.

~ ~ ~

The morning sun filtered through the tall windows of the library, casting long golden stripes across the floor. Madeline sat in the alcove beneath the window, her hands folded in her lap, her thoughts tangled like thread.

She had been summoned by her Father and she knew only too well why.

The door creaked open and her Father entered, his steps measured, his expression composed. He did not sit immediately, but walked to the hearth and stood with his back to her, gazing into the cold grate.

"I spoke with Monsieur de Villeroy yesterday," he said at last.

Madeline's breath caught. "I see."

"He is displeased," her Father continued. "He feels…neglected."

Madeline looked down. "Well I have been busy and I do not wish to see him."

Monsieur de Marais turned, his eyes narrowing slightly. "That is not your choice to make."

Madeline stood, her voice quiet but firm. "Then why give me a tutor who teaches me to think? To feel? To question?"

Her Father's jaw tightened. "Geneviève Rousseau is here to prepare you for your role. Not to unravel it."

"She is teaching me to understand myself," Madeline said. "And I am beginning to understand that I do not want this marriage."

Monsieur de Marais stepped closer. "You speak like a girl who has read too many novels. This is not a story, Madeline. It is your future and it has been arranged with care."

Madeline's voice trembled, but she did not look away. "Arranged for whom? For me? Or for the family name?"

Silence fell between them, heavy and unyielding.

Finally, her Father sighed. "Étienne will be returning today at noon. You will receive him."

Madeline's heart thudded. "And if I refuse?"

Monsieur de Marais looked at her, and for a moment, something flickered in his eyes - regret perhaps or the ghost of understanding.

"You will not," he said. "Because you are a de Marais. And we do not refuse what is expected."

He turned and left the room, the door closing behind him with a soft click.

Madeline remained by the window, the sunlight now warming her face. She felt the storm inside her rising again - but this time, it did not feel like fear. It felt like the beginning of something else.

~ ~ ~

There was a knock on Madeline's door as she sat at by the window staring into the gardens. She was not expecting anyone and it startled her from her gaze deep in thought.

"Enter"

Geneviève entered gracefully her presence immediately grounding Madeline.

They hadn't spoken since the lesson. Since touch had become truth.

"I'm so relieved to see you" Madeline said "Did you know he is coming today?"

Geneviève nodded. "Yes I'd heard." She walked closer and sat beside her, "And how do you feel?"

Madeline looked at Geneviéve intently, her eyes filled with fear and something fiercer. " I don't want to belong to someone who doesn't ask what I want."

"So you've told your Father how you feel - about your reservations?"

Madeline stared at the floor. "Yes, I said I don't want to but it was pointless, my Father has made clear to me what my responsibilities to this family are, in this arrangement. I feel like I'm walking into a storm. But I'm not sure if I'm the one being swept away…or the one conjuring it."

Geneviève smiled faintly. "Both, perhaps. Storms are not always destruction. Sometimes they clear the air."

Madeline looked up. "He will be angry that I have been avoiding him."

"Let him be," Geneviève said. "Anger is a mask for fear. And men like Étienne fear what they cannot control."

Madeline exhaled slowly. "I'm afraid this could turn out very badly.." Madeline searched Geneviéve's eyes desperately for answers.

Geneviève took her hand, "Madeline, I may have been employed by your Parents to prepare you for this marriage but it does not sit well with me to continue to push you into a situation you do not want to be in - we are talking about the rest of your life"

"No matter what the outcome, you will rise again and I will be here to support you"

Madeline felt relief run through her body - finally someone who was listening to her, listening to what she wanted.

CHAPTER SIX

The Meeting

The clock struck noon.

Madeline stood in the drawing room, her hands clasped tightly in front of her. She wore a pale pink gown - modest and elegant, again chosen by her Mother. Her hair was pinned, her posture perfect. But beneath the surface, her heart beat like a drum.

Étienne arrived precisely on time as always and with more roses. His coat was embroidered with gold thread, his boots polished to a mirror shine. He walked like a man who believed the world bent to his will.

"Madeline," he said, bowing slightly.

She curtsied, her movements automatic. "Monsieur."

"You've been difficult to reach? I trust your lessons are progressing."

Madeline's hands tightened. "Yes they are...enlightening."

He studied her. "Geneviève is thorough, I hear. But I wonder what kind of preparation keeps a bride from her betrothed."

Madeline met his gaze. "I suppose the kind that asks who she is before she becomes someone's wife."

He glanced at her. "Geneviève Rousseau is a curious choice. My

Mother says she was once a courtesan."

Madeline turned to face him. "Does that offend you?"

Étienne smiled, but it was thin. "Not at all. I believe experience is valuable. Especially in women who must serve."

Madeline's breath caught. "Serve?"

He looked at her sternly. "You will be my wife, Madeline. My partner, yes - but also my possession. I will protect you, provide for you and in return, you will obey."

She stared at him, the roses behind him blurring in her vision.

"I am not a possession," she said quietly.

Étienne's expression darkened. "You are what society allows you to be."

Madeline stepped back. "Then society is wrong."

He reached for her hand but she pulled away.

"You speak like a girl who's been misled," he said. "Perhaps Madame Rousseau is teaching you more than she should."

Madeline's voice trembled, but her words were clear. "She's teaching me to see myself and she's teaching me to understand myself."

He leaned forward. "You are not meant to understand yourself. You are meant to be a Wife. A lady. A Mother."

Madeline's voice was quiet but firm. "And what if I want to be more?"

Étienne stared abruptly. "This is foolishness. You are being led astray."

Madeline stated calmly, "No. I'm being led inward."

He stepped closer. "You are mine, Madeline. Promised and soon to be bound."

Madeline turned her head to look at him directly. As her eyes met his, there was no fear in them - only a quiet defiance.

She took a step back. "I was promised to you yes - but it was never my promise."

Étienne's eyes darkened. "Your Father will not will not go back on his word and your families honour - you speak like a woman who forgets her place."

Madeleine: "Perhaps I've never known it."

Étienne: "You'll learn. In time."

Madeleine: "Or you'll learn that I'm not yours to tame."

He stared at her, as if seeing her for the first time - not as a docile bride, but as a woman with a spine and a voice.

Étienne turned on his heel and left without another word - leaving the scent of roses and resentment in his wake.

Madeline stood alone in the drawing room, her breath shallow, her hands shaking.

But inside, something had settled.

She had faced him.

She had not broken.

And for the first time, she felt the shape of her own power.

~ ~ ~

Rain began to pour dawn outside - hitting the windows with intensity. The corridors blurred around her as she walked briskly her chest tight, her heart pounding. She didn't know where else to go. Instinct guided her feet toward the East Salon, though she had no invitation to go there.

She knocked quickly and when Geneviève opened the door a look of surprise flickered across her face, followed quickly by concern. "Madeline - what's happened?"

Madeline's composure crumbled. "I tried to explain," she said, breath unsteady. "He was angry when I tried to tell him you'd been teaching me to know myself - he called me foolish, said I don't know my place," She looked down at the ground, "and as I stood up to him and spoke my mind, all I was thinking of was you and… and.."

Geneviéve tilted her head slightly, "and what else?"

Madeline looked her in the eyes directly, "My feelings for you."

Geneviève's eyes softened, "You should be very careful what you say next Madeline…"

"I had to come," Madeline interrupted. "Because I can't pretend any longer. I feel for you what I have never felt for anyone. I don't understand it and I don't need to. I just know it's real and I want to know more"

There was silence - the kind that hums with everything unspoken.

Geneviève stepped closer, her restraint faltering. "You think I haven't fought the same battle?" she murmured. "From the first day, I knew I should keep my distance. Yet here you are and I can't send you away."

Madeline searched her face. "Then don't."

Geneviève hesitated only a moment more before reaching out - not as a teacher but as a woman who had finally surrendered to her own heart.

Their hands found each other first, trembling. Then Geneviève leaned in and Madeline felt the world narrow to the warmth of her breath, the soft press of lips that spoke what words never could.

The kiss was tender and intense, the beginning of something neither of them could turn back from, a kiss of recognition of two souls finding each other in a world that had never made room for them.

Madeline melted into Geneviève. The fire crackled louder, the rain tapping faster but inside, time held its breath.

When they parted, Geneviève cupped Madeline's face in her hands.

"You are not wrong," she said. "You are not broken. You are not alone."

Madeline closed her eyes, tears slipping down her cheeks.

"I've never felt more alive," she whispered.

CHAPTER SEVEN
The Storm Within

The next morning the storm had passed but the air still felt heavy. The garden was soaked, petals clinging to wet stone, vines sagging under the weight of rain. Geneviéve stood at her window, watching the sky clear in streaks of pale gold.

A servant knocked on the chamber door. As Geneviéve answered, the servant's eyes lowered. "Madame Rousseau, Monsieur de Villeroy requests your presence in the study."

Geneviéve's stomach turned. "Did he say why?"

"No, Madame. Only that it is urgent."

She followed the servant through the corridors, each step echoing louder than the last. The study door loomed ahead - dark wood, brass handle, silence behind it.

She knocked once.

"Enter," came the voice.

Étienne stood by the fireplace, his posture stiff, his gaze sharp. He didn't offer a chair.

"You've been spending a great deal of time with Madeline," he said.

Geneviève kept her voice calm. "She is my pupil."

"She is my Fiancée."

Geneviève met his eyes. "She is her own person."

Étienne stepped closer. "I've heard whispers. Servants talk. Doors creak. You think you're clever, but this house has eyes."

Geneviève didn't flinch. "Then let them see."

Étienne's jaw tightened. "You are poisoning her. Filling her head with fantasies. She was obedient before you arrived."

"She was silent," Geneviève said. "There's a difference."

He moved fast - grabbing her wrist, not hard but firm enough to make her catch her breath.

"If you continue teaching her in this manner I can have you removed," he said. "I've spoken to her Parents and I do have the power to make that happen."

Geneviève pulled her arm free. "You can dismiss me. But you cannot unteach what she's learned."

Étienne's voice dropped. "She will marry me and she will forget you."

Geneviève turned to the door. "If that's what you truly believe, then you don't know her at all."

She walked away, heart pounding, throat tight. The corridors blurred around her.

Back in her chamber, she found a note tucked beneath her pillow. Folded once. No seal.

"Come to the greenhouse tonight at Midnight after the Masquerade Ball."

She pressed it to her lips, eyes closed.

The storm had not passed. It had only begun.

CHAPTER EIGHT

The Masquerade

The ballroom shimmered with candlelight, its vaulted ceilings painted with cherubs and constellations. Music swelled from the quartet in the corner - violins and harps weaving a tapestry of sound that wrapped around the guests like silk.

Madeleine stood at the top of the grand staircase, her mask a delicate lattice of gold and pearls. Her gown was midnight blue, cinched at the waist, the neckline daring by her Mother's standards. She felt exposed, but powerful. Tonight, she was not a Daughter. Not a bride. She was a mystery.

Below, nobles danced and drank, their laughter echoing off marble. Masks concealed faces but not intentions. Whispers passed like wine - sweet, intoxicating, dangerous.

Geneviève appeared near the fountain, dressed in deep crimson her mask black velvet edged in silver. She moved through the crowd like smoke - flowing and elegant.

Madeleine descended slowly, her eyes locked on Geneviève's and her breath caught. When she reached the bottom, neither bowed. Neither curtsied. They simply stood, two women in a room full of roles they refused to play.

Geneviève offered her hand. "Dance with me."

Madeleine hesitated. "They will all see."

"They already do. They just don't know what they're seeing."

She took Geneviève's hand.

They moved to the edge of the ballroom, where shadows softened the rules. The music shifted - slower now more intimate. Their bodies aligned, hands resting where no one dared place them. Geneviève felt the heat of Madeleine's palm through her glove, the press of her waist beneath layers of silk.

They danced.

Not with steps taught by tutors, but with instinct. With longing.

Madeleine leaned in, her lips near Geneviève's ear. "I dreamt of you last night."

Geneviève's hand tightened. "And what happened in your dream?"

"We ran away together."

Geneviève pulled back just enough to meet her gaze. "Perhaps it was not a dream?"

A servant passed, eyes lingering too long. Geneviève looked away slightly, her heart pounding.

Geneviève's voice was low. "We must be careful."

"I don't want careful," Madeleine said. "I want real."

Geneviève touched her cheek, just once. "Then you must be brave."

The music ended. The crowd applauded. The masks remained.

But beneath hers, Madeleine was no longer hiding. She was choosing.

Madeleine stepped back from Geneviève, her breath shallow her skin tingling where Geneviéve's fingers had touched her, still holding each other's hand, reluctant to let the moment pass.

Applause rippled through the ballroom, polite and curious. A few masked faces turned toward them, but none dared speak.

Then came the sound of boots - measured, deliberate.

Étienne.

He emerged from the crowd like a blade unsheathed, his mask a sharp cut of ivory and gold, his expression unreadable beneath it. In his gloved hand, he held a single white rose.

"Madeleine," he said bowing with precision. "May I claim the next dance?"

Geneviève's hand slipped from hers, slow and deliberate. She did not bow. She did not speak. She simply stepped back into the shadows, her presence lingering like perfume.

Madeleine turned to Étienne. "Of course, Monsieur de Villeroy."

She placed her hand in his and he led her to the centre of the ballroom. The quartet began again - this time a stately minuet, all form and structure.

They danced.

Étienne's grip was firm, his steps exact. "You looked... spirited," he said. "With your tutor."

"She is not just my tutor," Madeleine replied. "She is my guide."

He narrowed his eyes. "She is dangerous."

"To whom?" Madeleine asked. "To you? Or to the version of me you prefer?"

Étienne's jaw clenched. "You are my betrothed. You owe me respect."

"I owe you nothing that was promised without my consent."

They turned, the dance forcing them into proximity, their faces inches apart.

"You humiliate me," he hissed. "In front of the court. In front of your Family."

"I reveal myself," she said. "If that humiliates you, perhaps you should ask why."

Étienne's hand tightened at her waist. "You forget your place."

Madeleine met his gaze, unflinching. "No. I am finally beginning to understand where I want it to be."

The music ended. They bowed.

He released her hand as if it burned him.

"Enjoy your rebellion," he said coldly. "It will not last."

He turned and walked away, the rose crushed beneath his feet.

Madeleine stood alone for a moment, the ballroom spinning with colour and sound. Then from the edge of the room, Geneviève appeared once more - silent, steady, waiting.

Madeleine did not return to her family. She did not retreat to the safety of the walls that had shaped her.

She walked toward the woman who had taught her to choose.

And this time, she did not look back.

CHAPTER NINE
The Secret Garden

The greenhouse stood at the far edge of the estate, half-hidden by ivy and shadow. Once a place for orchids and citrus, it had long been abandoned - its glass panes streaked with age, its air thick with the scent of damp earth and forgotten blooms.

They had agreed to meet there after the ball had finished.

Madeline with her cloak pulled tight against the chill, slipped through the side gate, heart pounding, breath visible in the moonlight.

Inside the air was warm. Lanterns flickered low, casting golden light across the overgrown vines and moss-covered stone. And there, standing amongst the wild roses, was Geneviève.

She no longer wore her mask. No pretence.

Geneviève stepped forward. "I was afraid you would not come."

Madeline reached out, brushing her fingers along Geneviève's cheek. "I would have come even if the world burned behind me."

Their lips met softly, then with urgency. Hands found skin, fabric fell away and the space between them vanished. They moved together like music - slow, deliberate, aching.

Geneviève guided Madeline to the bench beneath the hanging vines, her touch reverent, her gaze unwavering.

"You are not a girl anymore," she whispered. "You are a woman and you are mine."

Madeline trembled beneath her, not from fear, but from anticipation. She had never felt so alive, so claimed yet so free.

Their bodies spoke in gasps and silence, in the language of longing and defiance. Outside the wind stirred the leaves. Inside time unraveled.

Hands and mouths moved hungrily over each other in a rhythmic dance of passion.

Afterward, they lay entwined in each other, the lanterns dimming, the roses blooming around them like witnesses.

They did not speak for a long time.

Geneviève traced the curve of Madeline's shoulder. "If they find us..."

Madeline kissed her hand. "Then let them. I would rather be ruined with you than touched by anyone else."

Madeline closed her eyes, her head resting against Geneviève's chest.

In the greenhouse, surrounded by wildness and warmth, they were no longer tutor and pupil. No longer bride and mistress.

They were simply two women who had chosen each other.

~ ~ ~

The greenhouse was quiet now. The lanterns ceased to burn, the scent of jasmine lingering in the air like a memory. Geneviève sat alone on the stone bench, her fingers tracing the edge of a fallen petal.

Madeline had left just before dawn break, slipping back into the estate like a shadow. They had agreed it was safer but the silence felt heavier than any risk.

A rustle broke the stillness.

Geneviève turned sharply.

A figure stood at the entrance, young and slight, dressed in servant's garments. Eyes wide. Mouth parted.

"I - I didn't mean to intrude," the girl stammered. "I was sent to check the Greenhouse, someone saw lanterns on earlier."

Geneviève rose slowly. "What did you see?"

The girl hesitated looking down "I saw... someone. Two people. I didn't know it was you."

Geneviève stepped forward, her voice calm but firm. "You will say nothing. To anyone."

The girl nodded, but her eyes betrayed her. Fear. Curiosity. The kind that spreads.

Geneviève watched her disappear into the morning light, heart pounding.

She knew what was coming and by daybreak, the whispers had begun.....

~ ~ ~

Servants exchanged glances. A maid dropped a tray when Geneviève returned and entered the estate.

By midmorning, Madeline's Mother had summoned Madeline for tea. The drawing room was quiet, the fire low. Madeline entered without knocking, her heels sharp against the parquet floor.

"You embarrassed him last night," she said without preamble.

Madeline looked at her. "I told him the truth."

Her Mother's lips thinned. "Truth is not always useful, Madeline. Especially not for women in your position."

"And what position is that?" Madeline asked. "Silent? Obedient? Decorative?"

Her Mother's eyes flashed. "Respected. Soon to be married. Secure." She took a deep breath in and looked directly at Madeline, "Do you think I loved your Father when we wed? Stability is our gift to you - but love? Love is a luxury few ever experience."

Madeline stared at her with defiance, "Then if you've never known this luxury - I pity you."

Her Mother's hand twitched, as if tempted to strike but she only turned away. "You are playing a dangerous game."

"No," Madeline said softly. "That's what no one understands, I'm refusing to play one."

~ ~ ~

Later that morning when she couldn't find Geneviéve in her chambers - Madeline finally found her in the library, her expression drawn with worry in her eyes, an expression she'd never seen before.

"They know, someone saw us in the Greenhouse," Geneviève said as she stood up.

Madeline nodded. "I know." She said with a new found inner strength, "Do you regret it?"

Geneviève looked at her with sadness "No. But I fear what comes next. I fear they will send me away to stop this from progressing any further. In their eyes I'm ruining you and any chance of the future your Parents have arranged for you"

Madeline crossed the room, cupping her face. "If they send you away, I will come with you. I don't want what's been arranged for me - I want you. I've never been more certain of anything in my life."

Geneviève's eyes showed concern. "I'm afraid for you - more so than me."

Madeline kissed her gently. "I don't want to be afraid anymore, I'd rather be brave with you than safe without you."

Outside, the estate buzzed with rumours. Inside, two women stood together - defiant and in love but filled with hope.

The world for the first time, felt like a place they might actually have a chance of living in, on their own terms.

A knock shattered the quiet.

Geneviève opened the door to find a servant pale and trembling, looking down. "Madame Rousseau is summoned to the drawing room. Immediately."

Geneviève's jaw tightened. "By whom?"

"Monsieur de Villeroy. And Madame de Marais."

Madeline stepped forward. "I'll come with you."

Geneviève shook her head. "No. Go to my chamber. Whatever happens, stay there."

She kissed her quickly - fierce and protective as she disappeared down the corridor.

CHAPTER TEN

The Ultimatum

The drawing room was cold despite the fire. Étienne stood near the hearth, arms crossed. Madeline's Mother sat stiffly in a velvet chair, her expression carved from stone.

Geneviève entered without ceremony.

Étienne spoke first. "You've corrupted her."

Geneviève didn't blink. "She is not a child. She makes her own choices."

"You were meant to teach her to be my Wife," he snapped. "Not your indulgence."

Geneviève stepped closer. "I taught her how to recognise what she wants, to know herself and her own mind."

Madame de Marais stood and raised her voice, "That was not the lesson! You will leave this house today. If you do not, we will ensure you are ruined. Legally! Socially! Entirely!"

Geneviève's voice was calm. "I will leave but you cannot unteach what she's learned."

Étienne's eyes narrowed. "She *will* marry me. I have her Parents word."

Geneviève turned to Madame de Marais. "And you will let that happen? To your own Daughter? Let her live a miserable unfulfilled life that she doesn't want?"

"She is not the first woman to sacrifice desire for duty," her Mother said. "She will survive."

Geneviève's voice dropped. "Survive yes but she will not be living."

~ ~ ~

She returned to her chamber, heart pounding, hands shaking. Madeline was waiting, eyes wide, her cloak clutched around her.

"Your Mother has ordered me to leave," Geneviève said. "If I don't leave, I will watch you be forced into a life you didn't choose and they will ruin my name."

Madeline stepped forward. "Then we leave together."

Geneviève stared at her. "Are you certain you want to give up everything?"

Madeline nodded. "It was never mine to begin with and I never wanted it."

Geneviève pulled her into an embrace, their bodies fitting together like verses in a poem. They kissed - slowly, deeply, with the weight of decision pressing into every breath.

They undressed each other without words, each touch a vow. Geneviève traced the curve of Madeline's spine, kissed the hollow of her throat, whispered truths into her skin.

Madeline responded with urgency, with the kind of love that doesn't ask permission.

They made love as if the world had already ended. As if nothing remained but this - skin, breath, heartbeat.

Afterward, they lay in the sheets, the light shifting across their bodies.

Madeline whispered, "Where will we go?"

Geneviève kissed her temple, her eyes searching upwards "Somewhere they cannot follow."

Madeline smiled as she closed her eyes.

CHAPTER ELEVEN

The Departure

The sun had not yet risen, but the estate was already stirring. Footsteps echoed in distant corridors, shutters creaked open and the scent of baking bread drifted through the halls. But in Geneviève's chamber, time had slowed.

Madeline lay beneath the sheets, her bare skin warmed by the embers in the hearth and the lingering touch of Geneviève's hands. Her hair fanned across the pillow her eyes half-closed her body aching in the most exquisite way.

Geneviève sat beside her, fully dressed, her fingers lacing a small satchel shut. Inside: letters, money, a map, a pair of gloves. The essentials for escape.

Madeline stirred. "You're leaving without me?"

Geneviève turned, her expression soft. "Never. But I must go first. Secure the carriage. Pay the driver. Make sure no one follows."

Madeline sat up, the sheet falling to her waist. "I want to come with you."

Geneviève held Madeline's face, "You will. Tonight. When the house sleeps. I'll return for you."

Madeline reached out, tracing the line of Geneviève's jaw. "What if they try to stop us?"

Geneviève kissed her palm. "Then we run faster."

They sat in silence, the weight of goodbye pressing between them. Geneviève leaned in, her lips brushing Madeline's shoulder, then her collarbone, then lower, each kiss a promise, each breath a vow.

Madeline pulled her closer, her fingers slipping beneath the fabric of Geneviève's bodice. "Stay a little longer? Please?"

Geneviève hesitated, then nodded. She undressed slowly, deliberately, letting Madeline watch. Her body was strong, marked by time and tenderness. Madeline reached for her, and they met in the centre of the bed, limbs entwining like vines.

Their lovemaking was slower this time - with less urgency and more intention. Madeline traced every inch of Geneviève's skin, memorising the texture, the scent, the sound of her sighs. Geneviève responded with equal devotion, her hands and mouth worshipping Madeline's body.

They whispered to each other between kisses:

"I love you."

"I choose you."

"I will come for you."

Afterward, they lay enmeshed in silence, the sheets damp with sweat and tears. Geneviève rose first, dressing quickly, her movements efficient but reluctant.

She kissed Madeline one last time - deep, lingering, final.

"I'll be back at midnight," she said. "Pack only what you need. Leave everything else."

Madeline nodded, her throat tight. "I'll be ready."

Geneviève slipped out the door, her footsteps fading down the corridor.

Madeline sat alone in the quiet, the scent of her lover still clinging to the sheets. She rose slowly, crossed to the window, and watched the sky begin to lighten.

She would leave tonight.

She would not look back.

~ ~ ~

It felt like the longest day of Madeline's life waiting for nightfall, she had managed to avoid her Parents all day.

Finally night fell and the estate slept.

Candles had been snuffed, doors bolted and the last of the servants had retired to their quarters. Only the wind stirred the ivy along the stone walls, whispering secrets to the night.

Madeline stood in her chamber, dressed in a simple traveling gown - dark wool, no embroidery, no jewels. Her satchel was light: a change of clothes, a book of poetry, gold coins, a silver locket with her Mother's portrait. She left behind the rest. The dresses. The heirlooms. The life she had been groomed to inherit.

She opened the door slowly, heart pounding. The corridor was empty.

Geneviève had told her to wait until midnight. It was five minutes past.

Madeline crept down the hallway, her footsteps muffled by the thick carpet. She passed portraits of ancestors she no longer wished to resemble. At the end of the corridor, a door opened silently.

Geneviève stood there cloaked in black, her hair braided tightly her eyes sharp with purpose.

Madeline smiled. "You came back."

"I said I would." she whispered.

They didn't kiss. Not yet. The moment was too fragile, too urgent. Geneviève took her hand and led her through the servant's passage, down a narrow staircase and out into the garden.

The greenhouse loomed ahead, dark and wild. Beyond it, the carriage waited - hidden behind the hedges, the driver paid in coin and silence.

They reached the carriage without incident. Geneviève helped Madeline inside, then climbed in after her. The door shut. The wheels began to turn.

Only then did they breathe.

Madeline leaned into Geneviève, her head resting on her shoulder. "I thought they'd try to stop us."

"They still might," Geneviève said. "But at least we're already gone and we have a head start."

The carriage rattled over stones and dirt leaving behind the estate, the expectations and the lies. Madeline watched the trees blur past, her fingers entwined with Geneviève's.

"I'm scared," she said.

Geneviève kissed her temple. "So am I. But fear is not failure."

They rode in silence for hours, the moon rising high above the hills. When the carriage stopped for water and to rest the horses, Geneviève led Madeline into a nearby grove secluded, quiet, bathed in silver light.

There, beneath the trees, they kissed.

It was not hurried. It was not desperate. It was the kiss of two women who had chosen each other again and again, despite everything.

They undressed slowly, laying their cloaks on the grass. Their bodies met like poetry - soft, deliberate, aching. Madeline traced the lines of Geneviève's shoulder and back, she kissed the curve of her hips, whispering her name like a prayer.

Geneviève responded with devotion, her hands studying every inch of Madeline's skin, her mouth writing verses across her chest.

They made love beneath the stars, the wind rustling the leaves like applause.

Afterward, they lay tangled together, the earth beneath them, the sky above.

Madeline whispered, "Where will we go?"

Geneviève smiled. "Where no one knows our names. Where we can begin again."

Madeline closed her eyes. "I can't wait to begin my forever with you."

~ ~ ~ THE END ~ ~ ~

ABOUT THE AUTHOR

Gabrielle Wise is a writer of evocative sapphic fiction, exploring the intimate spaces where desire, identity and self-discovery intertwine. She has crafted a slow-burning lesbian romance set against atmospheric backdrops - from gilded estates to historical worlds rich with emotion and tension.

When she's not writing, Gabrielle is inspired by art, history and world travel which has inspired this deeply sensual book about forbidden love.

The Art of Desire is her debut novella.